THE GREAT GLUCOSATED LEAP

VOLUME I: THE SEMANTIC LIBERATION

RUBEN ALCOBA

Conceptual Prologue: A novel about the deconstruction of oppressive semantics and the ascent to power through philosophical density.

TABLE OF CONTENTS

INTRODUCTION

CHAPTER 1 THE EPISTEMOLOGY OF THE "WORKER"

CHAPTER 2 THE NATURAL CONCLUSION OF DECEPTION

CHAPTER 3 THE BACKSEAT RHETORIC

CHAPTER 4 THE EPIPHANY OF FROZEN MONEY

CHAPTER 5 HYDRIC DEMOCRACY AND THE PACHA MAMA

CHAPTER 6 THE SEMANTIC EXODUS TO BACU

CHAPTER 7: THE FORT LAUDERDALE VACUUM

CHAPTER 8 THE PROTEAN NATURE OF THE VECTOR

EPILOGUE THE TRILOGY OF THE SEMANTIC ENIGMA

DEFINITIONS THE SEMANTICS OF POWER

CONCEPTS FROM THE CRISIS (INTRODUCTION & CHAPTER 7):

CONCEPTS FROM EPISTEMOLOGY (CHAPTER 1)

EL TROPE'S SEMANTIC RESTRUCTURING DICTIONARY: CHAPTER 2 CONSOLIDATION

CHAPTER 3 THE BACKSEAT RHETORIC

CHAPTER 4 THE EPIPHANY OF FROZEN MONEY

CHAPTER 5 HYDRIC DEMOCRACY AND THE PACHA MAMA

CHAPTER 6 THE SEMANTIC EXODUS TO BACU

CHAPTER 7 THE VACÍO DE FORT LAUDERDALE (THE FORT LAUDERDALE VACUUM)

CHAPTER 8 THE PROTEAN NATURE OF THE VECTOR

EPILOGUE: THE TRILOGÍA DEL ENIGMA SEMÁNTICO (THE TRILOGY OF THE SEMANTIC ENIGMA)

EL TROPE ON THE DECONSTRUCTOR VS. REORGANIZER

INTRODUCTION

PART 1: THE GREAT GLUCOSATED LEAP

The mid-afternoon sun in Fort Lauderdale, Florida, was an assault on the cornea that President Rodolfo "El Trope" de Bianco considered a capitalist rudeness. Visibly fatigued and carrying twenty extra pounds due to a life dedicated to high-risk alimentary restructuring, El Trope was in a bar, fulfilling an urgent in-field sociological analysis, a presidential euphemism for getting drunk with dignity. His gaze, of an almost religious seriousness, fixed on the center of the makeshift dance floor: a young woman, in an act of pure Dionysian liberation, swaying on a table and a chair. As the rhythm saturated the atmosphere, El Trope, the president who had risen to power by restructuring the thirst of his people, did not see a dance move; he saw a philosophical crisis that only he could dismantle. He straightened up, adjusted his imaginary tie, and, with a grave and dense voice, began his Trope de Bianco Monologue:

"Compatriots of Bianco. What has been seen in this... digital footage, this dance, that people state is spontaneous, is not a simple fact of the nightlife scene. No. It is a profound manifestation. A sociological phenomenon that demands structural reading from us."

(Trope pauses dramatically, raising a finger.)

"We must ask ourselves: What is the vector of euphoria? What is the mechanism of Dionysian liberation that drives the youth to momentarily suspend the dialectic of reason for the kinetics of rejoicing?"

(Trope leans slightly forward, with a tone of intellectual conspiracy.)

"I tell you: this is not just music. This is the social interest rate that has overflowed. It is the historical deficit of leisure opportunities that translates into an excess of pelvic movement at night. Every step, every spin... is not a dance move, it is an act of resistance against the rigidity of the workday, against the neoliberal structure of boredom."

(Trope stands up again, with an air of solemn conclusion.)

"And let me be clear. The true problem is not the dance. The true problem is that, to reach such a level of corporal honesty, there has to mediate, I suspect, and I say this with the seriousness that characterizes me, an extraordinary accumulation of sugar and electrolytes, perhaps in the form of what you call a cocktail. It is the economics of sugar cane taken to its maximum danceable expression. We must, for the good of the nation, investigate the glucose content in these scenarios and determine if the bar's fiscal policy is promoting a high-risk energy sovereignty."

(El Trope nods slowly, convinced of his analysis.)

"The dance is a symptom. And the symptom demands a total reform of Bianco's party policy. Let it be said."

PART 2: THE SEMANTIC COUNTERATTACK: TROPE VS. THE "FASCISM OF SERIOUSNESS"

While President Trope was in a state his team officially categorized as in-field sociological analysis, Bianco's media machinery wasted no time. Traditional newspapers, anchored in what El Trope would call bourgeois reductionism, attacked him mercilessly:

- **EL HERALDO DE BIANCO** (Traditional Opposition): "El Trope: From Semantic Leader to Alcoholic Drunk! Who governs Bianco while the President analyzes other people's knees in a Fort Lauderdale bar?"

- **LA VOZ DEL ORDEN** (Conservative): "He's just an analyzing drunkard watching a dance. El Trope, in an act of intoxication, has dishonored the presidential office. The nation demands a sobriety test, not a sugar cane analysis."

The Chief of Communications, Sofia, who seemed to have aged five years in two weeks, and the Minister of Economy, whose face paled beneath his Caribbean skin tone, found themselves facing a high-complexity dilemma: how to defend an inebriated monologue without lying about the alcohol intake? The answer was simple: elevating his drunkenness to the category of dense philosophy.

PART 3: THE OFFICIAL COMMUNIQUÉ FROM THE PRESIDENCY OF BIANCO

Issued without the President, happily inactive, having to lift a finger, the communiqué was presented as an academic rebuttal to the superficial press attack:

Subject: Reply to the Media Distortion about the Geometry of Nightlife Leisure

The Presidency of the Republic of Bianco regrets the chronic superficiality with which certain traditional media outlets have approached our profound reflection on the recent and viral act of liberated corporal expression. It is not, as they insist, a mere analyzing drunkard watching a dance. It is an exercise in social hermeneutics. We have exposed the undeniable correlation between the deficit in public investment in leisure culture and the explosive manifestation of individual euphoria in privatized urban space.

Trope's Declaration (Cited in a Prophetic Tone): "What the press calls intoxication, I call the historical accumulation of youthful frustration that, upon encountering an elevated glucose level and the right rhythm, finds a kinetic escape valve. It is a class struggle danced out, compatriots. The youth are shouting with their knees at what we do not allow them to say in classrooms or on executive boards. And I, as Head of State, have an ethical obligation to read that corporal grammar."

Central Points of the Reply (Science and Absurdity):

On the sugar hypothesis (Glucose and Hegemony): It is imperative that the press investigate the leisure supply chain. Who profits from the mass sale of high-concentration sugar and alcohol beverages? It is the rentier structure, the same one that opposes our reforms to democratize joy and free time.

Dance as an economic indicator: We propose including the nightly pelvic movement index (IMPN) as a complementary indicator to the gross domestic product (GDP). A high IMPN is not proof of disorder, but of an unsustainable social tension seeking liberation. A government that ignores the hips of its youth is a government that ignores its productive future.

The soft coup of boredom: The criticism I receive for analyzing the dance is an attempt to distract the nation from the crucial debate: the right to happiness without additives. I will not allow the fascism of seriousness to forbid us from thinking about the human condition revealed between the tables of a bar.

El Trope de Bianco reiterates his commitment to the profound analysis of the everyday and calls on the people not to fall into the media traps that seek to silence critical thought on any manifestation of life in Bianco, no matter how rhythmic and sugary it may be.

PART 4: OUTCOME

Far from sinking, El Trope, thanks to the Backseat Rhetoric applied by his assistants, rose twenty points in the polls. He had transformed a personal crisis into semantic liberation for an entire generation.

CHAPTER 1: THE EPISTEMOLOGY OF THE WORKER

The Office of the Minister of Defense of Bianco smelled of cheap pine air freshener and sandalwood incense, a mixture that, for eight-year-old Timoteo, represented institutional peace. Timoteo was sitting on a pile of military folders that his mother, the Minister of Defense, had used as a makeshift seat. Sitting across from him at the main desk, the nation's President, El Trope, tapped slowly on a calculator that resembled one bought at a bazaar back in 1985.

Timoteo's mother, Minister Salomé (formerly known in certain nightly avenues as La Dinámica), wore an immaculate emerald-colored suit. Her transformation from lady of the night to lady of the cabinet after a mystical revelation during a red light was one of the greatest successes of Trope's spiritual rehabilitation policy. Salomé had dropped out of school in eighth grade for reasons not worth detailing, and her aversion to mathematics was legendary, but there she was: in charge of war finances.

"Mommy," Timoteo asked, struggling to balance on the folders. "At school, the teacher says that two plus two is four. And that a worker is someone who builds buildings. But the President says that a worker is a vector of dignity. What is the scientific truth?"

Salomé smiled with the wisdom of someone who had seen both sides of the coin. "Look, son," Salomé began, looking at El Trope, who was still in his calculating trance. "What they teach you in school is not science, they are social norms. And President Trope, he is a linguist of liberation."

El Trope looked up from the calculator, his round face (already with his extra twenty pounds) illuminated with self-satisfaction. "Exactly, Salomé. It is the deconstruction of oppressive semantics."

"Do you see, Timoteo?" his mother continued. "The President doesn't change reality; he changes the prism through which we see it. He says that if the word prostitute offends you, the solution is not to prohibit it, but to see it as a Professional Treaty of Universal Pleasantries. We take a letter from here, add an accent there, and suddenly, there is no longer offense. It is linguistic justice."

Timoteo, fascinated, addressed the President. "And the numbers, President? You say that if I follow the number seven to its natural conclusion it leads me to a river."

El Trope leaned over the desk with the intensity of a preacher. "Timoteo, my young friend! Numbers in school are dogmas. They believe that four is an end. No! Four is the beginning. If you add your age, eight, to mine, fifty, and Salomé's age thirty-five, you get ninety-three. If you multiply nine times three, you get twenty-seven. If you subtract two minus seven, you get minus five. You, see? Numbers lead you to negativity. But if you take the seven, the biblical number, the number of the week, and follow it... it guides you to the flow, to

11

the movement, to purity. And what is pure and flow? The river! The River of Reason. That is ontological mathematics, not simple storeroom arithmetic."

Salomé nodded with fervor, although her brain only processed the word river.

"And about your question, my love," Salomé said, hugging Timoteo. "Your teacher tells you that only the builder is a worker. The President taught me that if I, Salomé, stood on a corner and sold my body so that you could eat and have shoes, I was a worker of the State with a salary based on intimate services. And now that I am here, paying the bills for the tanks, I am still a worker of the State with a salary based on defense services. The tasks are only social norms created by men. But if they feed my son, those tasks are blessed by Almighty, because His love has no moral prejudices or dress code restrictions."

Timoteo remained silent, feeling that he had learned more about real life in five minutes than in an entire school semester. President Trope nodded in approval, his serious gaze already planning how to introduce ontological mathematics into Bianco's educational reform. The seed of the semantic revolution had been planted in Bianco's future.

CHAPTER 2: THE NATURAL CONCLUSION OF DECEPTION

Before he was known as El Trope, he was simply Rodolfo, a young man from Bianco who believed in the Holy Trinity of Effort: the full workday, honest sweat, and the unwavering faith that God, or at least the vector of decency, would give him his earned bread. His religiosity was simple: God was in the details, in the straight line a bricklayer draws with chalk, and in the structural integrity of a promise kept.

Rodolfo, the son of farmers who had cultivated the same arid land since the beginning of the Republic, was the personification of the protestant work ethic grafted onto the tropics. He believed that success was the natural conclusion of continuous and documented effort. If you worked hard, wealth was, arithmetically speaking, inevitable.

This faith shattered with the arrival of Dr. Eloquence, a politician with soft manners and a well-kept beard who promised to transform the lands of Bianco into an Edenic Garden of Faith. Dr. Eloquence did not talk about infrastructure or interest rates, but about collective destinies and the will of Almighty.

"Compatriots," Dr. Eloquence proclaimed in rallies that looked like revival masses, "Bianco's prosperity is not in the financial wealth that you possess, but in the heart. If we surrender our possessions as a structured act of faith to finance my Great National Project, God will bless this land with a harvest that is not only abundant, but mystically superabundant."

Rodolfo, who had always distrusted rhetoric that could not be quantified, watched as his parents and neighbors, exhausted by decades of effort without profit, fell like dominos before the promise. People did not want the scientific truth; they wanted the comfortable narrative of redemption. They wanted to believe that the harsh reality could be dissolved by the semantic magic of a well-dressed man.

The trauma was visceral. Rodolfo's parents invested every coin they owned, losing the family farm after six months, when the Edenic Garden turned out to be a pyramidal structure of social drainage and Dr. Eloquence temporarily disappeared with the mystical capital.

In the ruins of his childhood faith, Rodolfo had his first great political epiphany:

Realization 1: Inequality is normal. Not everyone is born with the same vector of opportunities. His parents' sweat was not worth the same as Dr. Eloquence's persuasive saliva.

Realization 2: Work is a variable, not a guarantee. Effort is a necessary condition, but rhetoric is a sufficient condition for success in Bianco.

Realization 3: Collective blindness. Most people do not follow logic, but dramatic conviction. If a lie is told with enough emotional intensity and with references to transcendent authority, it becomes a political fact. People want to be lied to if the lie is beautiful.

In that moment of bitter cynicism and deception; Rodolfo made his decision: if he could not defeat the structure of deception, he would get into its gears to understand its mechanics. He decided that to be better than the common person, he had to master the epistemology of power.

Two months later, and after a series of mysterious calls, Rodolfo was at the opulent entrance of Dr. Eloquence's new coastal mansion. He had accepted a job that would put him closer to his enemy than anyone else, right at the level of his boots.

"Rodolfo, right? Welcome," said Dr. Eloquence with a smile that could have sold ice to an Eskimo. "Your task is to keep this Cadillac immaculate. You will be the mobile extension of my philosophy. We will see each other daily. I like my employees to be men of faith."

And so, Rodolfo, the man who had lost everything because of the politician's misplaced faith, became the driver of the very machine that had stripped him bare, beginning his long journey toward the deconstruction of oppressive semantics that, years later, he would use to govern Bianco.

CHAPTER 3: THE BACKSEAT RHETORIC

The driver's seat of a Black Cadillac, with tinted windows and glacial air conditioning, became Trope's School of Advanced Semantics. His classroom was the rearview mirror, and his professor was Dr. Eloquence.

Rodolfo spent his days immersed in an observational silence, listening to the decomposition of truth in real time. He watched Dr. Eloquence Gift the Moon to foreign investors, then justify local famine with the nobility of sacrifice, and finally, he reassures his wife about a bank account with an ethical reorganization of assets. Dr. Eloquence did not lie; he simply restructured the existential orientation of the facts.

"Rodolfo," Dr. Eloquence would say, without looking up from his satellite phone, "have you noticed the difference between saying that the people are ruined and saying that the people are in a period of spiritual capitalization?"

Rodolfo, with his hands steady on the wheel, would monotonously reply: "The first is a material description, the second is a metaphysical reorientation, Doctor."

"Exactly!" the politician would exclaim. "The first demands money. The second demands patience. And patience, Rodolfo, is an unlimited resource that does not get reported by the comptroller's office. The same goes for the concept of responsibility. I am not responsible for the crisis. I am the catalyst agent of necessary pain to achieve post-secular glory. Do you see? The word changes the route of payment."

Through hundreds of trips, Rodolfo cataloged every rhetorical trick, every semantic twist, and every fallacious natural conclusion. He understood that power lay not in weapons or money, but in the manipulation of belief through language. Dr. Eloquence had stolen his family's farm, not with a rifle, but with the correct adverb at the precise moment.

He channeled his rage into an obsessive study of grammar. Rodolfo began to believe that if one could understand the internal architecture of words, how a letter could alleviate pain, or how an adjective could conceal a crime, one could neutralize their power. His great personal project was to create a new therapeutic dictionary for Bianco, where words that caused shame or pain would be deconstructed and reassigned to a vector of dignity.

One day, while Dr. Eloquence was ordering him to drive to a discreet helipad to escape a spontaneous demonstration, Rodolfo heard him complain to an assistant: "All these people are so basic, so common. They believe the world works with the binary logic of two plus two equals four. They have no imagination."

That phrase hit Rodolfo. Dr. Eloquence did not see the people as victims, but as structurally defective beings due to their lack of rhetorical imagination.

At that moment, Rodolfo made a silent oath: he would rise above the common ground, not to steal from the people like Dr. Eloquence, but to save them from the tyranny of literal truth by teaching them their own weapon: Linguistic Justice. He would use density, absurdity, and complex semantics to confuse Bianco's enemies and elevate the workers of the State, regardless of the protean nature of their labor.

Rodolfo, the driver, had finished his doctorate at the university of cynicism and was ready to graduate. All he needed was his first opportunity to apply Backseat Rhetoric to the masses.

CHAPTER 4: THE EPIPHANY OF FROZEN MONEY

The morning sun reflected on Dr. Eloquence's private helicopter, giving it an air of transcendent glory that Rodolfo had learned to despise. "Rodolfo, my faithful driver," said Dr. Eloquence, adjusting his sunglasses as his notoriously silent wife boarded the cabin. "We are leaving. A spiritual retreat in a place where the surface of the problem is only white sand. You have been the constant variable in my business life. Your service has been a lesson in stoicism."

He gave Rodolfo a shiny black credit card, with the solemnity of one who grants a blessing. "Take this. It is a symbol of my appreciation. Never expect anything from something tangible, Rodolfo. Money is an illusion of control. The truly valuable thing is my last piece of advice: use my words as a guide to your well-being. rhetoric is the real capital."

And with that, the helicopter ascended, carrying the structure of Bianco's deception toward unknown skies.

Rodolfo went directly to the most exclusive bank in the capital, the one that boasted impregnable financial architecture. He inserted the card into the ATM with a feeling of nausea. He did not believe in the illusion of control, but a positive balance would help restructure the economy of his subsistence.

The ATM, with a flashing red light that Trope interpreted as an electronic moral judgment, spat out the card. The message on the screen was concise and poetic: ACCOUNT FROZEN. ASSETS IMMOBILIZED.

The betrayal was clean, traceless. Dr. Eloquence, on his flight, had secured all his assets and, in the process, froze the card he had given Rodolfo as a symbol of his appreciation. The tangible was, as expected, corrupt.

As Rodolfo left the bank, analyzing the natural conclusion of his former boss's generosity, two burly men, dressed in shirts that screamed tasteless opulence, grabbed him by the arms, and unceremoniously threw him into the back of a dark sedan.

"You're Rodolfo," one growled. "The Doctor's driver."

Rodolfo, who had already passed his quota of trauma for the day, remained calm. "I am, in the strict sense of the term, the former automotive worker of Dr. Eloquence."

The trip ended at a hacienda with more security than the presidential palace. In a luxurious room, bathed in gold and velvet, sat the man Dr. Eloquence had forgotten: El Zar, a drug trafficker who ran in the shadows. El Zar was not well-known. He had always used Dr. Eloquence as an agent of visibility before society and the Church (whose leaders received juicy donations for charity that only enlarged their properties). Dr. Eloquence, in an act of supreme ignorance, had conned El Zar's mother for an unspecified amount of money, without knowing who he was robbing.

"Rodolfo," said El Zar, with a surprisingly calm voice, like the eye of a hurricane. "The Doctor stole my mother's money. And from you, he stole your financial expectation. We are, in essence, both victims of Dr. Eloquence."

El Zar expected to find a coward, an accomplice. He found a man who only spoke of the internal architecture of deception. Rodolfo explained to him, with his dense logic, how Dr. Eloquence had used Bianco's spiritual capital for his personal benefit, how the Church was the moral clearing house for the crime, and how the frozen card was a perfect metaphor for the betrayal.

Impressed by Trope's cynical depth, El Zar smiled. "You are not a driver, Rodolfo. You have immense potential. A man with empathy for the system."

To recover his mother's dignity and prove Rodolfo's value, El Zar intentionally unleashed a textbook social dilemma: he withdrew from the market a necessity, clean bottled water, causing an artificial shortage of clean bottled water. The goal was to expose the power vacuum left by Dr. Eloquence.

"Show me, Rodolfo, that your theories of language are good for something tangible," El Zar challenged. "The people are thirsty. If you, the man with no money and no name, can use rhetoric to restructure thirst, you will be my man. And yours will be the path to power."

Rodolfo looked at the dilemma. The thirst of his people was not a metaphor; it was a material description that returned him to the trauma of his childhood. Rodolfo, the man who had sworn to be better than the common person through rhetoric, felt a sharp sting of real responsibility. It was his first opportunity to transform theoretical cynicism into an act of social service. He left the capo's hacienda, not with a gun, but with an idea charged with semantic complexity. He was going to change the way Bianco talked about thirst.

CHAPTER 5: HYDRIC DEMOCRACY AND THE PACHA MAMA

Rodolfo left El Zar's hacienda feeling urgency, not to save lives, but to confirm his theory. The bottled water crisis was not a logistical problem, but a deficit in collective will. People did not understand that not drinking was a superior political act.

He walked toward the center of the city, where people were standing in endless lines under the sun. Amid despair, Rodolfo found an oasis of surreal calm: Salomé, his future Minister of Defense, was sitting on the ground, with a rosary in one hand and a half-empty bottle of water in the other, preaching the wisdom of scarcity to a small crowd.

"Salomé!" Rodolfo exclaimed, recognizing the woman he had met in a brief, albeit intense, encounter at a seminar on the economy of barter.

Salomé, the reformed former lady of the night, was now an evangelist of hydric control. She had arrived at the Natural Conclusion of her faith: unlimited consumption was an offense to the cosmos.

"Rodolfo, you've arrived," she said, "The problem, Rodolfo, is that the people do not understand the divine sacrifice. The water did not leave; the Power Above tells us that we have been hydric gluttons. We must return a little to the Pacha Mama so that she blesses us with the flow."

Rodolfo was shocked. His cynicism, his theory of the rhetoric of deception, met literal faith. He realized that he did not have to create a lie; he only had to formalize the collective lie that already existed. The people already believed in a superior force that controlled the water; he only had to give it the necessary academic jargon and political dimension.

"Salomé," Rodolfo said, grabbing a microphone from a nearby protest stand. "You are not wrong, you are incomplete. The problem is the democratization of hydric consumption at a subatomic level."

Rodolfo climbed onto a wooden box (which held the last dozen bottles of water) and the crowd, thirsty and desperate, turned toward him. Anticipation hung in the air.

"Compatriots of Bianco!" Rodolfo shouted, his dense and grave voice filling the square. "The water shortage is not a distribution failure; it is an imposed theological reflection."

He paused for effect, staring intently at an old man who coughed dramatically. "We have historically been irresponsible hydric consumers. We have drunk, without conscience, the same consumption that the rest of the planet drinks. That, friends, is a cosmic offense. The Power Above, which Salomé calls Pacha Mama, has told us: You cannot drink the same consumption of water as the rest, because you must return a little to her so that she blesses you with the flow."

The crowd was confused but mesmerized by the seriousness of his gaze. "Therefore," Rodolfo continued, gesturing with the hand that had previously held the frozen card. "I decreed that the solution is the structural reorganization of personal consumption. From today on, every citizen of Bianco will not drink water in terms of milliliters, but in terms of environmental commitment. Every sip is an act of faith. And the act of not taking one more sip is a strategic deferral that honors the Pacha Mama."

The speech continued for half an hour more, an impenetrable mix of economics, quantum physics, and evangelical faith. Rodolfo never promised water; he promised the dignity of controlled thirst. When he finished, people were exhausted, but no longer hysterical. They did not understand what he had said, but they understood the solemnity of the promise. If Rodolfo, the man who came from a humble community, spoke of the Pacha Mama and hydric compression, it had to be the truth.

At the end of the speech, Salomé climbed onto the box with him, tears in her eyes. "Rodolfo, you are a prophet of logic."

"No, Salomé," Rodolfo replied, with the satisfaction of a scientist who has confirmed a hypothesis. "I am a deconstructor of sensitivity. People don't need water; they need a convincing narrative about why they don't have it."

El Zar, who was seeing the scene from a nearby building, turned off his binoculars with a smile. Rodolfo had not only solved the crisis; he had ideologically restructured it. He had found his man. And Rodolfo, in turn, had found his right-hand woman, the only person willing to marry blind faith with the dense jargon of the new Republic of Bianco.

CHAPTER 6: THE SEMANTIC EXODUS TO BACU

El Zar was not a man of patience, but of strategic timing. He knew that the narrative of thirst, the hydric restructuring devised by Rodolfo, would only work if it were prolonged for a period of biblical purification. Fifty days were too long; twenty was insufficient. Forty days, the time of the flood and of fasting, was the perfect number for collective faith.

"Rodolfo," El Zar ordered, with the seriousness of an orchestra conductor. "You are going to Bacu. An island with fascinating logistical architecture. I need you to learn about container leadership and perceptual distribution. I will return you to Bianco as an Apostle of Abundance."

And so, Rodolfo spent 40 days on the island of Bacu, a fiscal and logistical paradise where the science of legal camouflage was the only law. His tutor, a Cold War veteran turned import/export consultant, taught him the most important lesson in international politics: the power of the changed letter.

"Look, Rodolfo," his tutor explained, pointing to a cargo manifest. "If you move Transfer of Assets (TDA), it may be deemed an unlawful payment. If I just change one letter and put Transfer of Liabilities (TDP), I am moving hidden debt, black money, from one authority to another. It is the same ship, the same box, the same ocean. But my accounting semantics transforms it from crime to a tax relief structure. It is the legal deconstruction of morality."

Rodolfo gained new insight. It was the validation of his entire philosophy: if you change the word, you change the natural conclusion of the action.

In Bacu, Rodolfo also discovered something else: the immediate benefit of socialism. He met a group of philosophers and doctors in exile, idealists who spoke of health as a structural right and the economy of empathy. Rodolfo saw an opportunity in them. If Dr. Eloquence used faith to take away, he would use dense philosophy and tangible goods to give.

At the end of the 40 days, Rodolfo, now known as Trope, returned to Bianco, not in Cadillac, but on a massive cargo ship. The entrance was a spectacle worthy of a biblical hero. The ship not only brought the latest reserves of bottled water from Bacu (a managed donation by El Zar), but also:

Long-term water: A simplified (but very well-financed) infrastructure plan to purify the local river.

Human capital: Ten doctors with foreign degrees and a retinue of structural philosophy leaders ready to install Wellness Restructuring Clinics.

The perfect narrative: Trope, thin, tanned, and with a new philosopher's beard, presented himself not as a politician, but as an agent of international distributive justice.

The people, exhausted by the nobility of thirst and accustomed to scarcity, suddenly found themselves with a structural abundance. It was a change in basic assumptions so violent that they could not process it. People not only had water; they had water that carried a blessing of social conscience.

The press, partly controlled by El Zar's interests, at once crowned him as the Hero of the Forgotten. Trope was not a politician: he was a phenomenon. The fact that he had never held public office was, ironically, his greatest credential, for he was not part of the establishment.

With El Zar's financial support (who recovered his mother's money and dignity, and gained an invaluable political asset, Trope), the silent blessing of the Church (which had received an ethical reorganization of assets from Bacu), and popular clamor, the nomination was inevitable. The headline of the progressive press summarized it best: "El Trope is the candidate of imagination. His inexperience is his only quantifiable virtue."

Rodolfo "El Trope" de Bianco, the former driver ruined by misplaced faith, was now in the presidential race. He had risen to power not through logic, but through the natural conclusion of deception mastered by the backseat rhetoric. His first official function as a candidate was to declare: "My campaign is a strike at literality. Let's vote for semantic liberation."

(Once elected, Trope became President.)

CHAPTER 7: THE FORT LAUDERDALE VACUUM

The Fort Lauderdale sun attacked the cornea of the president of Bianco, El Trope, with a violence he considered unnecessary. He was at a teak table on the presidential hotel balcony, debating the future of his Hydric Democracy with two of his Central American counterparts. One, the minimalist technocrat from Azulia, talked about the efficiency of blockchain for drinking water distribution. The other, the conservative caudillo from the Republic of Gárgola, who cited biblical verses about rain.

El Trope, already twenty pounds heavier than he had been at his best, felt visibly fatigued by the heat and the lack of structural depth of his colleagues. "Colleagues," El Trope decreed, sliding his water glass with a napkin, "We are debating the surface of the problem here. The problem is not the scarcity of water, but the epistemology of consumption. Water, as an element, is a common good. When we turn it into a commodity, we privatize the citizen's existential thirst.

And, frankly, when you, colleague Gárgola, invoke divine intervention, you are externalizing the political cost of the shortage. It is an irresponsible fiscal theology."

The technocrat from Azulia sighed, the caudillo from Gárgola crossed himself, and El Trope, feeling that he had exhausted the morning's philosophical debate, stood up with a slight gasp. "With your permission, I must attend a matter of high protean complexity. My body demands alimentary restructuring."

What happened next, or rather, the sequence of events that mediated between the consumption of a shrimp cocktail and his awakening two weeks later, is still a subject of intense debate at the Bianco History Academy. Official records only show that that night, El Trope was last seen at an establishment known as El Paraíso de la Tusa y El Baile (The Paradise of Heartbreak and Dance), performing a deep and detailed oral exegesis on the choreographic motivations of a young woman.

El Trope woke up with a sharp pain behind his eyes, a sensation his subconscious defined as the metabolic revenge of sugar cane. He was on the sofa in his office in the Presidential Palace of Bianco, fully dressed but covered by a travel blanket with the national coat of arms. The smell of strong coffee permeated the air.

Facing him were three of his closest assistants: Sofia, the Chief of Communications, who looked like she had aged five years; the Minister of Economy, whose face paled beneath his Caribbean skin tone; and his bodyguard, who was simply reading the horoscope with disconcerting calm. The only notable absence was that of Minister Salomé, who, according to Sofia, was attending a transcendental urgency on the southern border, a euphemism that usually meant she was performing a mystical purification rite to ward off the negative capital of an attempted coup.

"Good morning, President," Sofia said, with a dangerously leveled voice. "Would you like some coffee? It's an Arabic resistance, you'll need it."

El Trope blinked, trying to assemble the chronology. "Days? What day is it today? I remember... the hydric debate. Fort Lauderdale. The surface of the problem..."

The Minister of Economy sighed and drank from his own cup. "President, fourteen days have passed. Since you, in an act that we have officially categorized as an in-field sociological analysis, went viral."

El Trope sat up with a jolt, assimilating the word viral. "Viral? Has my speech on the privatization of thirst broken the barriers of media hegemony?"

"Something like that," Sofia continued, passing him a tablet with narrowed eyes. "The video of your ethical-analytical monologue about the dancing young lady broke the internet. Two weeks. You have been inactive. But your image has exploded. We have had to manage five diplomatic crises, deny three coup rumors, and, most importantly..."

The Minister leaned in and put a trembling hand on his shoulder. "You, President, the man who talks about the dialectic of reason and structural deficits... are now the official spokesperson for Bianco's Youth."

El Trope felt that the Arabic resistance was not enough. "The spokesperson? Me? For the youth? Why?"

Sofia slid the most recent progressive press headline to him.

EL TROPE: THE PROPHET OF THE PARTY HIS PROFOUND READING OF GLUCOSE IS THE NEW GENERATIONAL MANIFESTO

"Youth say that your analysis of the economics of sugar cane and kinetic resistance is the most real thing a politician has said in Bianco in the last fifty years," Sofia explained. "We have had to launch a line of merchandise. IMPN, my favorite indicator. And the bars love it. They call it the Glucosated Leap. Youth idolize you. They believe you are with them in the fight against the fascism of seriousness, as you called it."

El Trope, his gaze lost on the blanket with the national coat of arms, murmured, "So... the Dionysian liberation... turned out to be an effective communication strategy?"

The Minister of Economy nodded slowly. "You've gone up twenty points in the polls, President. And please, this afternoon you have a TikTok live with the leaders of the Influencer community to talk about designing public policies for the after-party."

El Trope took a long sip of coffee, the solemnity returning to his face. The weight of his new role was immense. "Good," he said, in a deep voice. "Then, if we are to address the structure of the party, we must do so with the intellectual rigor that Bianco demands. Bring me the latest WHO studies on the post-euphoric rehydration rate. The revolution does not stop, even if I did for two weeks."

CHAPTER 8: THE PROTEAN NATURE OF THE VECTOR

My dear reader, let us pause our ascent to the River of Reason and address a concept of fundamental structural integrity that frees us from the economic restrictions of the fascism of seriousness: The protean nature of dignity.

THE TYRANNY OF THE TANGIBLE

The common mind, the mind imprisoned by the Tyranny of Literal Truth, insists that dignity can only attach itself to the *tangible*: the brick, the harvest, the balance sheet. This mindset, born of the old order, is rooted in the tragic belief that if the labor is abstract or morally judged, the worker loses their status as a Worker of the State.

But what happens when the job itself is liquid? When necessary, action shifts its form every six months? When is the product not a commodity but a condition? To understand this, we must embrace the protean nature.

THE CONSTANT VECTOR, THE SHIFTING FORM

The term protean derives from the ancient nautical deity, Proteus, who owned the ultimate skill of existential reorientation: he could change his shape at will. This is not mere disguise, compatriot; it is the philosophical mastery of form over essence.

Protean nature is the characteristic of any action whose external, observable manifestation (its *form*) is volatile, adaptable, or morally judged, yet whose internal, dignified purpose (its *essence*) is still utterly constant.

According to Bianco, dignity means that a job is acceptable when it provides enough support for both the worker and their family.

The vector of dignity is constant.

The protean nature is the shape it takes.

THE LIBERATION OF LABOR

My Minister, Salomé, understands this truth better than any bureaucrat. Her labor's protean nature has shifted dramatically:

Form 1 (protean nature): Standing on a corner, selling services. The external form is intimate, judged by the world.

Form 2 (protean nature): Sitting in the Ministry, paying for tanks. The external form is defense, judged by the market.

Both forms, though wildly different in their protean nature, share the same dignified vector: feeding her son. Therefore, both are the work of a worker of the State.

The Workers of the future will thrive on this principle. His labor, the generation of third-party emotional stability, will be abstract, non-physical, and therefore entirely protean. His task is to generate a capital of social resilience, not bricks or numbers.

To be free, reader, you must accept that the form of your labor is irrelevant and that only its purpose matters. Embrace the protean nature and recognize that literalness is the true enemy of the State!

EPILOGUE: THE TRILOGY OF THE SEMANTIC ENIGMA

The press room at the Presidential Palace featured LED light rings, microphones in assorted colors, and a neon sign that displayed: BIANCO: The Vector of Dignity. El Trope, in his dark wool suit and polished philosopher's beard, sat facing three of Bianco's most important Influencers: CucharaFina (the gastronomic critique expert), DataQueen (the fitness and self-management guru), and El Sensei del Flow (the opinion leader of youth culture and the man who had popularized the term Glucosated Leap).

The TikTok live had over ten million simultaneous viewers. The audience, accustomed to Trope's dense rhetoric, but euphoric about his recent Dionysian liberation in Fort Lauderdale, expected a manifesto.

DataQueen, with an optimistic voice and measuring her words for the camera, posed the first question, the most obvious after the viral incident.

QUESTION 1: THE STRUCTURE OF CONTENT

DataQueen: "President, after your in-field sociological analysis became a global phenomenon, the metric of success has changed. In our creator economy, how do you define the success or intrinsic value of a piece of content? Is it virality, monetization, or something that goes beyond?"

El Trope took a sip from a glass that, according to his security personnel, held only purified water.

El Trope : "Excellent question, DataQueen. It attacks the surface of the problem. The intrinsic value of content, in the age of protean information, does not exist in the speed of its propagation (virality), nor in its translation to the tangible (monetization). These are mere kinetic symptoms. The value exists in its epistemological interference capacity. That is to say, the amount of cognitive dissonance it generates in the recipient. The most successful piece of content is the one that manages to make the consumer question, even for a nanosecond, if the binary logic of two plus two equals four is truly the natural conclusion of the Universe. The higher the degree of dissonance, the more successful its interference. Its success is directly proportional to its capacity to destabilize the mental status quo."

CucharaFina blinked twice as he placed his hand thoughtfully against his chin. DataQueen simply nodded slowly, but her brain was struggling with the concept that engagement was the measurement of doubt.

El Sensei del Flow, the youngest of the three, and the closest to after-party culture, addressed the topic of work.

QUESTION 2: THE FUTURE OF THE WORKER

El Sensei del Flow: "President, you said in Chapter 1, that all citizens who feed their families are Workers of the State, regardless of their protean nature. But in today's world, where jobs change every six months, what is the vector of dignity for the worker of the future? What task counts as structural labor if it is not tangible?"

El Trope leaned forward, his gaze fixed on the camera.

El Trope: "The vector of dignity has not changed since the beginning of the Republic. Only its geometric manifestation is different. The error is to keep tying dignity to tangible production: the brick, the cultivation, the assembly. The worker of the future will not be a producer of objects, but a manager of collective inner peace. The most important and necessary labor in Bianco is the generation of third-party emotional stability. The influencer who alleviates the loneliness of a young person, the therapist who restructures trauma, the artist who challenges monotony; all of them are laborers of inner peace. Their work, although it does not generate a physical product, generates a capital of social resilience infinitely more valuable than any metal. Their salary is not for what they do, but for the emotional deficit they manage to mitigate in the nation."

The Influencers looked at each other, processing the idea that their work was, in fact, a mitigation of national depression and not just product advertising.

Finally, CucharaFina, the most traditional, decided to go straight to the core of politics.

QUESTION 3: THE ESSENCE OF GOVERNANCE

CucharaFina: "President Trope, you have reached the presidency without a traditional political career. What, then, is the true function of governance? Is it law, justice, or the national budget? What makes your system the River of Reason?"

El Trope smiled for the first time in the entire interview, a smile that seemed more like a conceptual diagnosis than an expression of joy.

El Trope: "Law, justice, and the budget are, as we have established, the surface of the problem. The true function of governance is the management of the narrative of collective acceptance. Governing is nothing more than the constant application of ontological mathematics. If you have a problem (say, the number 7, scarcity) and the people insist on seeing it as a negative end, my job is to restructure its logical trajectory so that the natural conclusion is not panic, but the River of Reason. I do not make laws; I reorganize the semantics that frame them. If people accept the narrative, the law becomes redundant. My system, friend, is the philosophical compression of collective will."

El Trope stood up, finishing his coffee. "In summary," he concluded, "I do not govern Bianco; I edify the reality of Bianco."

The three Influencers were speechless, with TikTok cameras capturing every moment and viewers flooding the comments with a whirlwind of emotions. They had asked for a headline and had received a doctoral thesis.

El Trope left the set, leaving his communications team to deal with the interpretation crisis. Minister Salomé was waiting outside, with an expression of mystical pride.

"Rodolfo," she said, "no one understood a word. It was glorious!"

"I know, Salomé," Trope replied. "Semantic liberation is a slow process. The people of Bianco still need to understand that literality is the true enemy of the State."

And with that, President Trope de Bianco headed to his office, his mind already occupied with the Logical Architecture of the next step, leaving behind a country dependent on his Ontological

Mathematics and three promising themes for the saga of *The Great Glucosated Leap*.

DEFINITIONS: THE SEMANTICS OF POWER

The following glossary defines the core concepts and terms used by President Rodolfo "El Trope" de Bianco throughout the narrative. These definitions, often convoluted, are the foundation of his philosophical platform: the deconstruction of oppressive semantics and the implementation of Linguistic Justice.

CONCEPTS FROM THE CRISIS (INTRODUCTION & CHAPTER 7):

Trope's Term (Original Spanish)	Literal Meaning (English)	Trope's Conceptual Translation (English)	Example of Usage (Based on Text)
Análisis Sociológico en Campo	Sociological Analysis in the Field	Presidential euphemism for "getting drunk with dignity" and fulfilling an urgent study on "the geometry of nightlife leisure". Officially, the event was cataloged as this by his staff to counter media attacks.	"The President is currently unavailable; he is fulfilling an urgent in-field sociological analysis in Fort Lauderdale, which resulted in him being inactive for fourteen days."
	Liberación Dionisíaca	Dionysian Liberation	The kinetic mechanism of rejoicing. A pure,

41

Trope's Term (Original Spanish)	Literal Meaning (English)	Trope's Conceptual Translation (English)	Example of Usage (Based on Text)
			corporal expression of freedom seen in a dancing young woman that suspends the dialectic of reason.
Neoliberal Structure del Aburrimiento	Neoliberal Structure of Boredom		The rigid framework of the workday and the deficit of historical leisure opportunities against which youthful dancing is an act of resistance.
Economía de la Caña de Azúcar	Economics of Sugar Cane		Trope's analysis of the market structure that promotes the "mass sale of high-concentration sugar and alcohol beverages" to fuel "Dionysian liberation".

Trope's Term (Original Spanish)	Literal Meaning (English)	Trope's Conceptual Translation (English)	Example of Usage (Based on Text)
	Soberanía Energética de Alto Riesgo	High-Risk Energy Sovereignty	The dangerous state created when a bar's fiscal policy promotes an "extraordinary accumulation sugar and electrolytes."
	Hermenéutica Social	Social Hermeneutics	The deep, academic-level interpretation of a social phenomenon (like dancing) that goes beyond "bourgeois reductionism".
	IMPN	Nightly Pelvic Movement Index	An indicator complementary to the GDP, used to measure an unsustainable social tension that seeks liberation.
	Fascismo de la Seriedad	Fascism of Seriousness	The attempt by critics (the media, opposition) to distract the nation

Trope's Term (Original Spanish)	Literal Meaning (English)	Trope's Conceptual Translation (English)	Example of Usage (Based on Text)
			from the crucial debate: the right to happiness without additives.
Retórica del Asiento Trasero	Backseat Rhetoric		Trope learned the entire system of power and manipulation of belief while driving for El Doctor Eloquence. Used by his assistants to successfully spin his scandal.
Liberación Semántica	Semantic Liberation		The deconstruction of oppressive semantics to transform a personal crisis into a positive outcome for an entire generation. The core philosophical goal of the movement.

Trope's Term (Original Spanish)	Literal Meaning (English)	Trope's Conceptual Translation (English)	Example of Usage (Based on Text)
	Teología Fiscal Irresponsable	Irresponsible Fiscal Theology	The act of invoking divine intervention (citing scripture on rain) to externalize the political cost of the shortage.

CONCEPTS FROM EPISTEMOLOGY
(CHAPTER 1)

Trope's Term (Original Spanish)	Literal Meaning (English)	Trope's Conceptual Translation (English)	Example of Usage (Based on Text)
	Trabajador	Worker	A vector of dignity; any citizen whose task, regardless of its "protean nature," feeds their family.
	Lingüista de la Liberación	Linguist of Liberation	Trope's self-defined role as one who does not change reality but changes the prism with which we see it.
	Deconstrucción de la Semántica Opresiva	Deconstruction of Oppressive Semantics	The philosophical process of dismantling language that causes pain, shame, or restriction, making it the central theme of the novel.

Trope's Term (Original Spanish)	Literal Meaning (English)	Trope's Conceptual Translation (English)	Example of Usage (Based on Text)
Justicia Lingüística	Linguistic Justice		The re-engineering of offensive words by "taking a letter from here, adding an accent there" so that there is no longer offense.
Matemática Ontológica	Ontological Mathematics		The system where numbers are not dogmas but guides to philosophical concepts. Used to plan how to introduce the concept in Bianco's educational reform.
Río de la Razón	River of Reason		The destination of Ontological Mathematics; the philosophical flow and movement that stands for the purity of the correct conclusion.

Trope's Term (Original Spanish)	Literal Meaning (English)	Trope's Conceptual Translation (Englis)	Example of Usage (Based on Text)
Santísima Trinidad del Esfuerzo	Holy Trinity of Effort	The naive, pre-Trope belief system based on full workday, honest sweat, and the faith that decency would bring earned bread.	"Before the deception, Rodolfo believed in the Holy Trinity of Effort: if you worked hard, wealth was, arithmetically speaking, inevitable."
	Ética Protestante del Trabajo injertada en el trópico	Protestant Work Ethic Grafted onto the Tropics	The belief that success is the natural conclusion of continuous and documented effort, a belief Trope's family held.

Trope's Term (Original Spanish)	Literal Meaning (English)	Trope's Conceptual Translation (Englis)	Example of Usage (Based on Text)
Jardín Edénico de la Fe	Edenic Garden of Faith		The metaphorical, mystically superabundant promise made by "Eloquence" that served as a pyramidal structure of social drainage.
Acto de Fe Estructurado	Structured Act of Faith		The rhetorical device used by Eloquence to convince citizens to surrender their possessions.
Capital Místico	Mystical Capital		The collective wealth invested by the citizens based on faith, which "Eloquence" disappeared with.
Epistemología del Poder	Epistemology of Power		The knowledge of *how* power works, specifically how it is rooted in rhetorical manipulation and the

Trope's Term (Original Spanish)	Literal Meaning (English)	Trope's Conceptual Translation (Englis)	Example of Usage (Based on Text)
			structure of deception.
	AutoridadTrascendente	Transcendent Authority	A reference, often spiritual or divine, used in conjunction with emotional intensity to convert a lie into a political fact.

Trope's Term (Original Spanish)	Literal Meaning (English)	Trope's Conceptual Translation (English)	Example of Usage (Based on Text)
Santísima Trinidad del Esfuerzo	Holy Trinity of Effort	The naive, pre-Trope belief system based on full workday, honest sweat, and the faith that decency would bring earned bread.	"Before the deception, Rodolfo believed in the Holy Trinity of Effort: if you worked hard, wealth was, arithmetically speaking, inevitable."
	Ética Protestante del Trabajo injertada en el trópico	Protestant Work Ethic Grafted onto the Tropics	The belief that success is the natural conclusion of continuous and documented effort, a belief Trope's family held.
	Jardín Edénico de la Fe	Edenic Garden of Faith	The metaphorical, mystically superabundant promise made by "Eloquence" that served as a

Trope's Term (Original Spanish)	Literal Meaning (English)	Trope's Conceptual Translation (English)	Example of Usage (Based on Text)
			pyramidal structure of social drainage.
	Acto de Fe Estructurado	Structured Act of Faith	The rhetorical device used by Eloquence to convince citizens to surrender their possessions.
	Capital Místico	Mystical Capital	The collective wealth invested by the citizens based on faith, which "Eloquence" disappeared with.
	Epistemología del Poder	Epistemology of Power	The knowledge of *how* power works, specifically how it is rooted in rhetorical manipulation and the structure of deception.
	Autoridad Trascendente	Transcendent Authority	A reference, often spiritual or divine, used in conjunction with emotional

Trope's Term (Original Spanish)	Literal Meaning (English)	Trope's Conceptual Translation (English)	Example of Usage (Based on Text)
			intensity to convert a lie into a political fact.

CHAPTER 3: THE BACKSEAT RHETORIC

Trope's Term (Original Spanish)	Literal Meaning (English)	Trope's Conceptual Translation (English)	Example of Usage (Based on Text)
Escuela de Semántica Avanzada	School of Advanced Semantics	The metaphorical "classroom" where Trope obtained his "doctorate in the university of cynicism", found in the back of the Cadillac.	"The seat of the driver became Trope's School of Advanced Semantics; his professor, Eloquence."
	Reorientación Existencial de los Hechos	Existential Reorientation of Facts	The technique used by Eloquence to avoid lying; he simply re-structures the facts to change their fundamental meaning.
	Capitalización Espiritual	Spiritual Capitalization	The rhetorical reframing of financial ruin or poverty, which

Trope's Term (Original Spanish)	Literal Meaning (English)	Trope's Conceptual Translation (English)	Example of Usage (Based on Text)
			demands "patience" instead of money.
	Agente Catalizador del Dolor Necesario	Catalyst Agent of Necessary Pain	The dignified, reframed role of a corrupt politician (like Eloquence) who is not "responsible" for a crisis, but for bringing about post-secular glory.
	Giro Semántico	Semantic Twist	Any rhetorical maneuver used to manipulate belief through language and change the route of payment.
	Nuevo Diccionario Terapéutico	New Therapeutic Dictionary	Trope's personal project aimed at creating a new language for

Trope's Term (Original Spanish)	Literal Meaning (English)	Trope's Conceptual Translation (English)	Example of Usage (Based on Text)
			Bianco, where painful words would be deconstructed and reassigned to a vector of dignity.
Tiranía de la Verdad Literal	Tyranny of Literal Truth		The structural defect of "common" people who work using the binary logic of two plus two equals four, which Trope sought to save them from.

CHAPTER 4: THE EPIPHANY OF FROZEN MONEY

Trope's Term (Original Spanish)	Literal Meaning (English)	Trope's Conceptual Translation (English)	Example of Usage (Based on Text)
Gloria Trascendente	Transcendent Glory	The deceptive visual aura given by the morning sun reflecting on Eloquence's private helicopter, which Trope had learned to despise.	"The sun reflected in the helicopter, giving it an air of Transcendent Glory, which Trope had learned to despise."
Variable Constante	Constant Variable	The contradictory, yet Stoic, role Trope was assigned by Eloquence in his life of business.	"You have been the constant variable in my life of business. Your service has been a lesson of stoicism."
Ilusión de Control	Illusion of Control	Eloquence's final advice to Trope, saying	"Never expect anything from

Trope's Term (Original Spanish)	Literal Meaning (English)	Trope's Conceptual Translation (English)	Example of Usage (Based on Text)
		that tangible wealth, like money, is merely a deceptive construct.	something tangible, Trope. The money is an illusion of control. The truly valuable thing is my last piece of advice: use my words as a guide."
Juicio Moral Electrónico	Electronic Moral Judgment	Trope's interpretation of the red light flashing on the ATM screen, signifying the bank's condemnation of the frozen card.	"The teller, with a flashing red light that Trope interpreted as an Electronic Moral Judgment, spat out the card."

Trope's Term (Original Spanish)	Literal Meaning (English)	Trope's Conceptual Translation (English)	Example of Usage (Based on Text)
Extrabajador Automotriz	Former Automotive Worker	Trope's immediate, linguistically restructured self-designation upon being apprehended, avoiding the common label of "The Doctor's driver".	"Soy, in the strict sense of the term, the former automotive worker of Dr. Eloquence."
Estructura de la Ofensa	Structure of Offense	The philosophical common ground between Trope (stolen financial expectation) and El Zar (theft committed against his mother), which binds them together	"The Doctor stole my mother's money and dignity. And from you, he stole your financial expectation. We are both victims"

Trope's Term (Original Spanish)	Literal Meaning (English)	Trope's Conceptual Translation (English)	Example of Usage (Based on Text)
		against Eloquence.	
Capital Espiritual de Bianco	Spiritual Capital of Bianco	The collective faith and trust of the nation, which Eloquence exploited for his personal benefit.	"Trope explained how Eloquence had utilized the Spiritual Capital of Bianco for his personal benefit."

CHAPTER 5: HYDRIC DEMOCRACY AND THE PACHA MAMA

Trope's Term (Original Spanish)	Literal Meaning (English)	Trope's Conceptual Translation (English)	Example of Usage (Based on Text)
VoluntadColectiva	Collective Will	The political factor lacking in the people that caused them to not understand that not drinking was a superior political act during the water crisis.	"The crisis was not a logistical problem, but a deficit in the Collective Will. The people did not understand that not drinking was a superior political act."
	Glotones Hídricos	Hydric Gluttons	The state of citizens who have been irresponsible hydric consumers by drinking the Same Consumption as the rest of the planet.
	Democratización del Consumo Hídrico a	Democratization of Hydric Consumption at the Subatomic Level	Trope's pseudo-scientific jargon for framing the water crisis is not as scarce, but as a

Trope's Term (Original Spanish)	Literal Meaning (English)	Trope's Conceptual Translation (English)	Example of Usage (Based on Text)
	Nivel Subatómico		deep structural problem requiring philosophical correction.
	Reflexió Teológica Impuesta	Imposed Theological Reflection	Trope's reframing of the water shortage, arguing that the crisis is a spiritual judgment from the "Power Above" (Pacha Mama) on the people's consumption habits.
	Mismo Consumo	Same Consumption	The cosmically offensive, irresponsible amount of water the people of Bianco were drinking, equating their intake with the rest of the planet.

Trope's Term (Original Spanish)	Literal Meaning (English)	Trope's Conceptual Translation (English)	Example of Usage (Based on Text)
	Compromiso Ambiental	Environmental Commitment	The new unit of measurement for water consumption, replacing the literal measurement of milliliters, thereby transforming a material need into a virtue.
	Diferimiento Estratégico	Strategic Deferral	The political act of not taking a drink (one more sip), which honors the Pacha Mama and shows Environmental Commitment.
	Profeta de la Lógica	Prophet of Logic	Salomé's immediate, admiring label for Trope after his speech, although Trope corrects her, calling himself a

Trope's Term (Original Spanish)	Literal Meaning (English)	Trope's Conceptual Translation (English)	Example of Usage (Based on Text)
			"reorganizer of sensitivity".
Deconstructor de la Sensibilidad	Deconstructor of Sensitivity		Trope's self-defined role as one who confirms his cynical hypothesis: people do not need water; they need a convincing narrative about why they do not have it.

CHAPTER 6: THE SEMANTIC EXODUS TO BACU

Trope's Term (Original Spanish)	Literal Meaning (English)	Trope's Conceptual Translation (English)	Example of Usage (Based on Text)
Purificación Bíblica	Biblical Purification	The strategic, rhetorical time (40 days) needed for the narrative of the water crisis (*Hydric Restructuring*) to work, aligning with the time of the flood and fasting.	"The narrative of thirst only works if it is prolonged during a period of Biblical Purification of exactly forty days."
Liderazgo de Contenedores	Container Leadership	The logistical skill Trope was sent to Bacu to learn, encompassing the science of camouflaging legal activity and the distribution of belief.	"You must go to Bacu to learn about Container Leadership and Perceptual Distribution."
Distribución Perceptiva	Perceptual Distribution	The skill of controlling how the movement	"You must learn about Perceptual

Trope's Term (Original Spanish)	Literal Meaning (English)	Trope's Conceptual Translation (English)	Example of Usage (Based on Text)
		of goods is perceived, a key part of Container Leadership learned in Bacu.	Distribution, where the real capital is rhetoric, not the goods themselves."
La Letra Cambiada	The Changed Letter	The most important lesson of international politics he learned in Bacu: how changing a single letter in a legal document transforms an action from a crime to a fiscal relief structure.	"By changing 'Transfer of Assets' (TDA) to 'Transfer of Liabilities' (TDP), you are using The Changed Letter to transform a possible crime into a structure of tax relief."
Socialismo del Beneficio Inmediato	Immediate Benefit of Socialism	The philosophical realization that the people will follow a leader who uses dense philosophy *and*	"If Eloquence used faith to take, Trope would use the Immediate Benefit of Socialism

Trope's Term (Original Spanish)	Literal Meaning (English)	Trope's Conceptual Translation (English)	Example of Usage (Based on Text)
		tangible goods to give, contrasting with Eloquence's faith-based theft.	dense philosophy plus tangible goods—to give."
Abundancia Estructural	Structural Abundance	The radical, overwhelming shift in paradigm experienced by the people when Trope returned from Bacu with water, doctors, and a new narrative, moving beyond scarcity.	"The people, accustomed to scarcity, suddenly encountered a magnificent Structural Abundance that they could not process."
Agente de la Justicia Distributiva Internacional	Agent of International Distributive Justice	Trope's self-defined role upon returning from Bacu, presenting himself not as a politician, but as a neutral force that restores balance.	"Trope presented himself not as a politician, but as an Agent of International Distributive Justice, thin, tanned, and

Trope's Term (Original Spanish)	Literal Meaning (English)	Trope's Conceptual Translation (English)	Example of Usage (Based on Text)
			with a new beard of philosopher."

CHAPTER 7: THE FORT LAUDERDALE VACUUM

Trope's Term (Original Spanish)	Literal Meaning (English)	Trope's Conceptual Translation (English)	Example of Usage (Based on Text)
Epistemología del Consumo	Epistemology of Consumption	The philosophical problem underlying the water debate, arguing that the issue is not logistical, but is rooted in *how* we know and justify consumption.	"The problem is not the logistics of water, but the epistemology of consumption. When we turn water into a commodity, we privatize the existential thirst."

Trope's Term (Original Spanish)	Literal Meaning (English)	Trope's Conceptual Translation (English)	Example of Usage (Based on Text)
Sed Existencial del Ciudadano	Existential Thirst of the Citizen	The profound, unstated need of the populace that is "privatized" when a common good, like water, is converted into a commodity.	"When we convert water into a commodity, we privatize the existential thirst of the citizen."
Reestructuración Alimentaria	Alimentary Restructuring	Trope's formal, philosophical term for his personal and public diet and consumption of food and drink, used to justify his weight gain and his trip to the bar.	"Visibly fatigued and with twenty pounds of weight extra products of a life surrendered to the alimentary restructuring of high risk." "My body demands an alimentary restructuring."
Venganza Metabólica de la Caña de Azúcar	Metabolic Revenge of the Sugar Cane	Trope's physical interpretation of his hangover; the consequence of	"El Trope woke up with a pain that his subconscious

Trope's Term (Original Spanish)	Literal Meaning (English)	Trope's Conceptual Translation (English)	Example of Usage (Based on Text)
		engaging in the Glucosated Leap and the Economics of Sugar Cane.	defined as 'the metabolic revenge of the sugar cane'."
Arábica de Resistencia	Arabic Resistance	The strong coffee Sofia, the Chief of Communications, offers the President to help him assemble the chronology after his two-week disappearance.	"The President felt that the Arabic Resistance was not sufficient for his new role."
Diseño de Políticas Públicas para el After-Party	Design of Public Policies for the After-Party	The surreal, high-level task Trope's staff assigns him, a TikTok live with Influencers, to embrace his new identity as the "Spokesperson for Bianco's Youth".	"You have a TikTok live with the leaders of the community of influencers to talk about the design of public policies for the after-party."

Trope's Term (Original Spanish)	Literal Meaning (English)	Trope's Conceptual Translation (English)	Example of Usage (Based on Text)
Tasa de Rehidratación Post-Eufórica	Post-Euphoric Rehydration Rate	The academic, scientific metric Trope demands studies on, showing his commitment to applying intellectual rigor to the analysis of the structure of the party.	"Bring me the latest studies of the WHO on the post-euphoric rehydration rate. The revolution does not stop."

CHAPTER 8: THE PROTEAN NATURE OF THE VECTOR

Trope's Term (Original Spanish)	Literal Meaning (English)	Trope's Conceptual Translation (English)	Example of Usage (Based on Text)
Naturaleza Proteica	Protean Nature	The characteristic of any action whose external, observable manifestation (its form) is volatile or morally judged, yet whose internal, dignified purpose (its essence) is still constant.	"The Protean Nature is the philosophical mastery of form over essence; it is what allows a worker to change their shape at will."
Vector de Dignidad	Vector of Dignity	The constant, pure, and unchanging internal purpose of labor: the task is	"The Vector of Dignity for a worker is simple and pure: the task is blessed if it

Trope's Term (Original Spanish)	Literal Meaning (English)	Trope's Conceptual Translation (English)	Example of Usage (Based on Text)
		blessed if it provides for the worker and their family. The opposite of the Protean Nature (which is the external form).	provides for their family."
Trabajador del Futuro	Worker of the Future	A person whose labor is abstract, non-physical, and entirely protean, such as the Manager of Collective Inner Peace.	"The Worker of the Future will thrive on the principle that the form of labor is irrelevant; only its purpose matters."
Propósito/Finalidad Digna	Dignified Purpose/Finality	The ethical essence of labor, which, according to Trope,	"The tasks are only social norms created by men. But if

Trope's Term (Original Spanish)	Literal Meaning (English)	Trope's Conceptual Translation (English)	Example of Usage (Based on Text)
		should be the sole determinant of a worker's value, making moral prejudice and dress code restrictions irrelevant.	they feed your son, those tasks are blessed by Almighty because his love has no prejudices, only Dignified Purpose."

EPILOGUE: THE TRILOGY OF THE SEMANTIC ENIGMA

Trope's Term (Original Spanish)	Literal Meaning (English)	Trope's Conceptual Translation (English)	Example of Usage (Based on Text)
Economía de Creadores	Creator Economy	The modern commercial system where the traditional metric of	"In our creator economy, how do you define the success of a piece of content? It is its

Trope's Term (Original Spanish)	Literal Meaning (English)	Trope's Conceptual Translation (English)	Example of Usage (Based on Text)
		success (monetization, viral speed) must be replaced by the value of Epistemological Interference.	capacity to generate cognitive dissonance."
Capacidad de Interferencia Epistemológica	Epistemological Interference Capacity	The intrinsic value of content, which is measured by the amount of cognitive dissonance it generates in the recipient; success is proportional to the content's ability to destabilize the mental status quo.	"The value resides in its Epistemological Interference Capacity. The most successful content is the one that makes the consumer question the logic of two plus two equals four."

Trope's Term (Original Spanish)	Literal Meaning (English)	Trope's Conceptual Translation (English)	Example of Usage (Based on Text)
Capital de Resiliencia Social	Capital of Social Resilience	The infinitely valuable, non-physical product generated by the Gestor de la Paz Interior Colectiva. It is the mitigation of the national emotional deficit.	"The Capital of Social Resilience is generated by the influencer who alleviates loneliness; it is infinitely more valuable than any metal."
Gestor de la Paz Interior Colectiva	Manager of Collective Inner Peace	The essential, dignity-restoring role of the worker of the future, who is not a producer of objects but a laborer of Generation of Third-Party Emotional Stability.	"The worker of the future will be a Manager of Collective Inner Peace; their salary is for the emotional deficit they mitigate in the nation."
MatemáticaOntológica	Ontological Mathematics	Trope's system of	"To Govern is the constant

Trope's Term (Original Spanish)	Literal Meaning (English)	Trope's Conceptual Translation (English)	Example of Usage (Based on Text)
		governance: restructuring a problem's logical trajectory so the Natural Conclusion is the River of Reason, not panic.	application of Ontological Mathematics. I do not make laws; I reorganize the semantics that frame them."
Gestión de la Narrativa de la Aceptación Colectiva	Management of the Narrative of Collective Acceptance	The true function of governance: the constant application of Ontological Mathematics to ensure the people accept the restructured reality, making laws redundant.	"The true function of governance is the Management of the Narrative of Collective Acceptance. If the people accept the narrative, the law becomes redundant."
Edificar la Realidad de Bianco	To Edify the Reality of Bianco	Trope's ultimate, profound	"I do not govern Bianco; I edify the reality of Bianco."

Trope's Term (Original Spanish)	Literal Meaning (English)	Trope's Conceptual Translation (English)	Example of Usage (Based on Text)
		definition of his presidential role, suggesting he is the architect of the nation's accepted existence.	

El Trope's Interviewees: Future Semanticists of Bianco

Trope's appearance transformed these Influencers from mere marketers into philosophical architects. Here are their satirical resumes, predicting their own literary or political careers following their exposure to Trope's density:

1. DataQueen: (The Guru of Dissonance)

a. Former Focus: Fitness, Autogestión, & Optimization.

b. Post-Trope Motto: "The engagement is the measurement of the doubt."

c. Future Book Title: *The Epistemology Digital of Dissonance: How Uncertainty is the Moneda del Siglo XXI*

d. Trope's Observation: Transformed her metric of success from monetization to Epistemological Interference Capacity. Her brain struggled, but her slow nod confirmed her subconscious conversion to the thesis that high dissonance equals high value.

2. El Sensei del Flow: (The Kinetic Mitigator)

a. Former Focus: Youth Culture, After-Party Dynamics, & Trend Leadership.

b. Post-Trope Motto: "My labor is the Generation of Third-Party Emotional Stability."

c. Future Book Title: *Capital de Resiliencia: Hacia una Economía Post-Servicio Basada en la Mitigación Emocional*

d. Trope's Observation: The most relevant to the Gran Salto Glucosado crisis. He was elevated from a social trendsetter to a Manager of Collective Inner Peace, realizing his work was not simple advertising, but mitigation of the national depression.

3. CucharaFina: (The Traditionalist of the Literal)

a. Former Focus: Gastronomic Critique, Caloric Content, and Material Aesthetics.

b. Post-Trope Motto: "The law, justice, and the budget are merely the surface of the problem."

c. Future Book Title: *Beyond the Calorie: The Philosophical Compression of the National Dish* (Unwritten, due to residual cognitive dissonance)

d. Trope's Observation: The firmest believer in tangible measurement (beauty of a dish measured in caloric content). His first bewilderment made him the perfect foil, forcing Trope to articulate the Management of the Narrative of Collective Acceptance.

EL TROPE ON THE DECONSTRUCTOR VS. REORGANIZER

My dear reader, let us pause this magnificent journey toward Semantic Liberation and address a question of fundamental epistemological gravity: Why, during a national water crisis, did I not label myself a mere Reorganizer of the liquid assets? Why, indeed, did I choose the far more structurally satisfying title of Deconstructor of Sensitivity?

The answer, compatriot, lies in the Tyranny of Literal Truth, the very enemy I swore to dismantle!

THE DEFICIENCY OF THE REORGANIZER

A Reorganizer is a functionary of the Surface of the Problem. He is the pitiable bureaucrat who believes that if the planning chart is messy, a new folder will solve the crisis. He works with the tangible: the bills, the pipelines, the milliliters.

The Reorganizer of the water system would promise you more water. This is an act of Irresponsible Fiscal Theology.

The Reorganizer is confined by the binary reasoning that two plus two always equals four. He lacks the rhetorical imagination necessary for true governance.

He is an amateur. He believes the problem is the *shortage*.

My role, learned in the Escuela de Semántica Avanzada (The School of Advanced Semantics A/K/A the backseat of the Cadillac), is not to manage the scarcity, but to manage the belief of the scarcity.

THE GLORY OF THE DECONSTRUCTOR

The Deconstructor of Sensitivity, by contrast, is a Linguist of Liberation and an artist of philosophical compression.

My goal was to expose the Estructura de la Ofensa (The Structure of the Offensive Language), which means that I must first deconstruct the very idea that *scarcity should cause panic*. I must convince the people that their discomfort is not a logistical failure, but an imposed theological reflection!

I deconstruct the need: I replace the material measurement (milliliters) with a moral one (environmental commitment). I tell them they are not thirsty; they are fulfilling a strategic deferral.

I deconstruct the guilt: I label them Hydric Gluttons, thereby justifying the shortage as a spiritual lesson from the Pacha Mama.

I deconstruct the symptom: I confirm that the people do not need water; they need a convincing narrative about why they do not have it.

A reorganizer fixes the *thing*. A Deconstructor fixes the *mind*. And in Bianco, as I learned from the expert manipulator, rhetoric is the real capital.

Therefore, I am a Deconstructor, one who dismantles the public's sensitivity to material reality, and only then can the glorious natural conclusion lead us to the River of Reason.

Any other label would be, quite frankly, a capitalist rudeness.

ADDENDUM TO THE RECORD

What you have read is not the collapse of a system. It is the moment it learned to preserve itself.

In this volume, language was still loud. Power still requires explanation. Truth was inconvenient, but it had not yet become evidence.

That phase is now complete. What follows is not persuasion, but containment.

In Volume II, speech no longer liberates. It incriminates.

The mechanisms introduced here are no longer argued; they are assumed. Rhetoric no longer performs. It withdraws.

Silence becomes the dominant architecture. Not because nothing is happening, but because everything is.

Volume II: *The Useful Silence* records what appears after semantic victory, when meaning no longer defends itself
and governance no longer explains.

The record is open.

www.ingramcontent.com/pod-product-compliance
Lightning Source LLC
Chambersburg PA
CBHW040743250626
47164CB00006BA/160